My Secret Unicorn

Twilight Magic

Linda Chapman

Illustrated by Ann Kronheimer

PUFFIN

PUFFIN BOOKS

Published by the Penguin Group

Penguin Books Ltd, 80 Strand, London WC2R ORL, England

Penguin Group (USA), Inc., 375 Hudson Street, New York, New York 10014, USA

Penguin Group (Canada), 90 Eglinton Avenue East, Suite 700, Toronto, Ontario, Canada M4P 2Y3
(a division of Pearson Penguin Canada Inc.)

Penguin Ireland, 25 St Stephen's Green, Dublin 2, Ireland (a division of Penguin Books Ltd)

Penguin Group (Australia), 250 Camberwell Road, Camberwell, Victoria 3124, Australia
(a division of Pearson Australia Group Pty Ltd)

Penguin Books India Pvt Ltd, 11 Community Centre, Panchsheel Park, New Delhi – 110 017, India

Penguin Group (NZ), cnr Airborne and Rosedale Roads, Albany, Auckland 1310, New Zealand
(a division of Pearson New Zealand Ltd)

Penguin Books (South Africa) (Pty) Ltd, 24 Sturdee Avenue, Rosebank, Johannesburg 2196, South Africa

Penguin Books Ltd, Registered Offices: 80 Strand, London WC2R ORL, England

www.penguin.com

First published 2006

017

Text copyright © Working Partners Ltd, 2006
Illustrations copyright © Ann Kronheimer, 2006
All rights reserved

The moral right of the author and illustrator has been asserted

Typeset in Bembo by Palimpsest Book Production Limited, Polmont, Stirlingshire

Made and printed in England by Clays Ltd, St Ives plc

British Library Cataloguing in Publication Data
A CIP catalogue record for this book is available from the British Library

ISBN-13: 978-0-141-32025-0

www.greenpenguin.co.uk

MIX
Paper from
responsible sources
FSC™ C018179

Penguin Books is committed to a sustainable
future for our business, our readers and our planet.
This book is made from Forest Stewardship
Council™ certified paper.

To Poppy and Kitty Young

CHAPTER

One

The night air felt cool against Lauren's arms as she ran down the dark path to Twilight's paddock. Above her, the stars were twinkling brightly in the clear sky.

A perfect night for flying, Lauren thought. She smiled. She was so lucky! Although Twilight, her pony, looked just like any other small grey pony, he was really a unicorn in disguise. Every night when Lauren said the magic Turning Spell he changed into his true form and then he could talk, do magic and fly.

Lauren knew Twilight wasn't the only secret unicorn. In fact, there were unicorns disguised as ponies all over the world. Each unicorn was supposed to find a special human friend to help them change into their magical shape and then they did good deeds together. Lauren and Twilight had helped lots of people and animals since she had first found out that he was a unicorn.

Tonight there was someone else who needed their help. Lauren speeded up. What would Twilight say when she told him her plan?

Twilight whinnied as she ran up to the gate.

'Hi, boy,' Lauren panted. 'We've got a

job to do tonight!' She quickly said the
Turning Spell.

'Twilight Star, Twilight Star,
Twinkling high above so far.
Shining light, shining bright,
Will you grant my wish tonight?
Let my little horse forlorn
Be at last a unicorn!'

With a bright purple flash, Twilight's
grey coat became snow-white, his mane
and tail grew and shone silver in the
starlight and a long horn appeared on
his forehead. He was a unicorn once
again!

'Hello, Lauren,' he said, nuzzling her.
'Does someone need our help?'

'Yes. It's Buddy,' Lauren replied. Buddy
was her brother Max's Bernese mountain
dog. 'He's really miserable because Max
has gone to stay with some friends who
live in the city. He's never been away for
more than a night before, and Buddy is
missing him so much! He won't eat or
play or do anything.'

'I thought he looked quiet when I

saw your dad taking him for a walk today,' Twilight said. 'But what can we do to help him?'

'I thought you could tell him that Max will be home in a few days,' Lauren explained. 'I don't think he understands that Max has just gone on holiday; I think he's afraid that Max has gone away forever. If you could tell him what's happening, maybe he'd feel happier.'

Twilight nodded. 'It's worth a try. But is it safe to let him see me when I'm a unicorn?'

'I was wondering that,' Lauren admitted. Until now she and Twilight had been careful not to let Buddy see Twilight in his magical shape in case the dog started acting strangely around Twilight. No humans were allowed to know about Twilight's secret, and Lauren didn't want to risk her parents or Max finding out. 'But Buddy's not a puppy any more. I'm sure if we explain that he mustn't let anyone know your secret, he'll understand that he has to act as if you're just an ordinary pony.' She sighed. 'I know it's a bit risky but I really want to help him.'

'Me too,' Twilight agreed. 'Let's do it!'

Lauren ran back to the house. Twilight had said just what she was hoping he would.

Buddy looked up from his bed when she came into the kitchen but he didn't woof. He was used to Lauren creeping in and out of the house at night.

'Come on, Buddy,' she whispered.
'Walk!'

Usually Buddy leapt around madly at
the prospect of a walk but now he just
got heavily to his feet and walked over.
He licked Lauren's hand in a subdued
way. He really wasn't his usual bouncy
self at all. Hoping her plan would work,
Lauren took hold of his collar and led
him out of the house.

When Buddy reached the field and
saw a unicorn standing by the fence, he
stopped dead and tilted his head to one
side, looking very surprised.

'It's OK, Buddy,' Lauren soothed
him. She climbed over the fence and

Buddy followed her, shuffling under
the railing.

Twilight snorted in greeting and
touched Buddy with his horn. 'Hello,
Buddy. It's just me, Twilight.'

Buddy's ears pricked up as he looked
at Twilight curiously.

'I'm a unicorn,' Twilight told him.

'But you mustn't let anyone know. Not even Max.'

At the mention of Max's name, Buddy's ears and tail drooped. He whined miserably.

Twilight understood what he was saying. He could talk to all kinds of animals when he was a unicorn, and they could talk back to him. 'No,' Lauren heard him say to the young dog. 'You've got it wrong. Max hasn't gone away forever, Buddy. He's just on holiday for a few days. He *is* coming back.'

Buddy's ears pricked up again. He barked, and to Lauren it sounded just as if he was saying 'Really?'

'Yes,' Twilight promised. 'Max will be

home in just a few days.' He glanced at
Lauren. 'You were right. Buddy *did* think
Max had gone forever.'

'Oh, Buddy,' Lauren said, ruffling the
dog's fur. 'Max would never abandon
you. He loves you.'

Twilight repeated her words to Buddy.

'Woof!' Buddy barked. Suddenly he
looked like a different dog. Bounding
away, he stopped and crouched down,
wagging his tail.

'I think he wants us to play chase!'
Twilight said.

Lauren grinned. 'What are we waiting
for?'

She ran after Buddy with Twilight
trotting beside her. With his mouth open

wide in a doggy grin, Buddy raced in
circles around them.

At last Lauren stopped, puffing and
out of breath. 'OK, come on, Buddy,' she
said. 'Time to take you back inside.'

Giving a quiet woof goodbye to
Twilight, Buddy trotted beside Lauren

up the path. When they reached the
kitchen, he ran over to his bowl and
polished off the biscuits he had left
earlier. Then he lay down in his bed
with a contented sigh.

'See you later, boy,' Lauren whispered,
shutting the door.

Happiness glowed through her as she
ran back to the field. She loved using
Twilight's magic to help people and
animals. Having a unicorn was just great!

'Thanks for explaining things to
Buddy,' she said to Twilight as she climbed
over the fence. 'I'm so lucky to have you.'

'I'm the lucky one,' Twilight said.
'You're a wonderful unicorn friend.'

'Me? I don't really do anything,'

Lauren protested. 'It's your magic that solves things.'

Twilight looked at her in surprise. 'That's not true. You do just as much as me.'

'No, I don't,' Lauren said modestly.

'You do,' Twilight insisted. 'Think of what happened tonight. I talked to Buddy but it was your idea. You were the one who realized that he needed someone to explain things to him.'

'I suppose so,' Lauren said slowly.

'You're very special,' Twilight told her.

Blushing, Lauren changed the subject. 'Are you looking forward to tomorrow? It's going to be fun, isn't it?'

Twilight nodded and swished his tail.

The next day Lauren had arranged to meet up with her two best friends, Mel Cassidy and Jessica Parker. They were going to ride over to Orchard Stables, a local livery stables which was owned by the mother of their friend Grace. One of her mares had just had a foal and Lauren, Mel and Jessica were going to

go and see it. Afterwards they were
going to take a picnic lunch to the
creek.

'I can't wait to see Currant,' Lauren
told Twilight. 'That's what Grace and her
mum have called the foal.' She smiled.
'I'm glad it's the holidays – we'll be able
to visit him lots. As well as doing all
kinds of other fun stuff, of course.'

Twilight pushed her with his nose.
'How about we start by going flying?'

'Cool!' Lauren said. Taking hold of his
mane she scrambled on to his back.
'Let's go to the woods and jump over
the tree tops.'

Twilight soared into the air. 'Sounds
good to me!'

CHAPTER
Two

The following morning, Lauren was fastening Twilight's girth when she heard the sound of hooves. Turning, she saw Mel and Jessica riding towards her on their ponies, Shadow and Sandy.

'Hi, Lauren! Are you ready?' Mel called.

'Almost.' Lauren checked Twilight's girth was tight, and mounted. 'Have you brought your lunch?' she asked, riding over to meet them.

Jessica patted a saddlebag behind her leg. 'Yep, here it is. Shall we go through the woods or across the fields?'

'Across the fields,' Lauren said. 'It's much quicker.' Orchard Stables bordered on to Lauren's dad's farm and he had said it was fine for them to ride around the edges of the fields.

As they rode down a tractor track, Lauren looked around at the ears of young spring wheat waving in the breeze. Overhead the sky was blue and the sun was shining. She sighed happily. 'Isn't it great to be riding instead of being at school?'

Mel nodded. 'No maths, no dumb
projects. No more Jade Roberts!'

Lauren grinned. Jade Roberts was in
their class at school. She was always
boasting about the prizes she had won
on her pony, Prince. She used to tease
Mel because Shadow hadn't been a very

good jumper. That is, until Lauren and
Twilight secretly helped him to
overcome his fears. What's more, Jade
had once owned Twilight but she'd sold
him to the Fosters because she didn't
think he was showy enough. *Luckily for
me*, Lauren thought, stroking Twilight's
mane. Jade hadn't cared enough about
Twilight to find out his magical secret!

Then she forced herself to push all
thoughts of Jade out of her mind. It was
far too nice a day to think about
someone who was so annoying! 'Shall
we canter?' she called to the others.

'Yes!' they replied together.

They clicked their tongues and the
three ponies surged forward eagerly.

With the breeze blowing in their faces, the girls cantered towards Orchard Stables.

The yard seemed very busy when they arrived. There were people everywhere, carrying rugs and tack and leading ponies.

'I wonder what's going on,' said Mel.

'Let's ask Grace,' Lauren said, seeing a tall slim girl with blonde hair hurrying out of the barn with a stack of buckets. She waved.

'Hi!' Grace called. Dumping the buckets by the water trough she came over. 'Have you come to see Currant?'

Lauren nodded. 'If it's still OK.' She glanced around. 'It looks pretty busy around here.'

'There are six new liveries arriving today,' Grace replied. 'Fox Run – the livery stables on the other side of town – is closing down and quite a few of the owners have decided to bring their horses here. It's great for Mum to have the business but it does mean it's going to be crazy today. Mum's in the tack room sorting things out and I've been trying to make sure the loose boxes are ready.'

'Do you want a hand?' Jessica offered.

Grace smiled. 'Thanks. It would be great to have some more help.'

Lauren, Mel and Jessica tied their ponies to a hitching rail and followed Grace to the tack room. There was stuff everywhere! Rugs, saddles, bridles and grooming kits were piled up all

over the floor. Grace's mum was
sorting through them with Jo-Ann,
Grace's best friend.

'Hello, girls,' said Mrs Wakefield. 'If
you've come to see Currant, I'm afraid
you'll have to wait a while. I have to
get this tack room sorted out first.' She

ran a hand through her short blonde
hair. 'It could take some time!'

'Would you like us to help?' Lauren
said.

Mrs Wakefield's face lit up. 'That
would be very kind, thank you!'

'What should we do?' Mel asked.

'If you could take the rugs into the
rug room and hang them up for me that
would be a great help,' said Grace's
mum.

Lauren, Jessica and Mel set to work.
With three of them working together
it didn't take long. Soon the rugs were
hanging up tidily in the rug room,
outdoor rugs on one rug rack, indoor
rugs and sweat sheets on another.

Meanwhile, Mrs Wakefield and Jo-Ann had hung up the saddles on saddle racks and sorted out the hats, boots and bandages into piles.

'Here are the last two rugs,' Lauren called, carrying two heavy New Zealand rugs across the yard for Jessica and Mel to hang up.

As they started draping the rugs over the racks, they heard the sound of raised voices outside.

'That stable on the corner is supposed to be for my pony. You'll have to move!'

'But I was here first!'

'Well, obviously no one told you it was reserved for my pony, Prince!'

Lauren's eyes flew to meet Mel's and Jessica's. There was no mistaking that bossy voice.

'It's Jade Roberts!' she cried.

CHAPTER
Three

Lauren, Mel and Jessica hurried to the doorway.

Jade was standing in the middle of the yard, glaring at a younger girl. 'Go on, move your pony out so I can put Prince in.'

Looking upset, the younger girl began to lead her pony out of the stable.

Jade smiled smugly. As she turned

away, she caught sight of Lauren, Mel and Jessica. 'What are you three doing here?' she asked.

'We could ask you the same question,' Lauren replied.

Jade tossed back her shoulder-length brown hair. 'I've just moved Prince here. We were at Fox Run until it shut down.'

Lauren's heart sank. That meant if they came to see Grace and Jo-Ann they'd probably end up bumping into Jade as well.

'So, why are you here?' Jade asked them curiously. 'You're not moving your ponies here as well, are you?'

'No,' Jessica answered. 'We just rode over to see Mrs Wakefield's new foal.'

'A foal?' Jade echoed, looking interested. 'How old is it?'

'Just a few days,' Mel replied.

'Cool,' Jade said. 'Where is it? I want to see it too.'

As she spoke, Mrs Wakefield came out of the tack room with Grace. 'Ah, someone else who wants to see Currant,'

she said, smiling. 'Well, why don't you join us, Jade? Now the tack room's done, I can take you all over to the foaling stable.'

'I'll come too,' said Grace. 'Currant's going to be mine when he gets older,' she told them proudly as they headed across the yard.

Her mum nodded. 'That's right. Grace
is going to help me break him in.'

'How do you break a horse in?'
Lauren asked.

Before Mrs Wakefield could reply, Jade
piped up. 'I helped my cousin break in a
pony last summer. It was great. I was the
first person to ride him because my
cousin's seventeen and a bit big for him.
You might have heard of my cousin,' she
said to Grace and her mum. 'She has
eight horses and does lots of show
classes with them. Her name's Maggie
O'Donald.'

'I have heard of her. She wins a lot.'
Mrs Wakefield looked impressed. 'It must
have been a great experience for you,

helping someone like that break in a pony.'

'It was,' Jade said. 'I know I'm *really* lucky.'

Lauren rolled her eyes at Mel and Jessica. Jade always acted sugary sweet around adults. She only showed her other side when there were no grown-ups around.

'I'm afraid you won't be able to touch Currant and Apple,' Mrs Wakefield warned them as they approached the foaling stable. 'Although Apple, Currant's mum, is usually really gentle, she seems to be feeling very protective of her new baby. I don't want to upset her or risk anyone getting hurt, so you'll just have

to look at Currant and not touch him.
OK?'

They all nodded.

The foaling stable was a single large
stable set on its own, away from the
main barns. Compared to the hustle and
bustle of the yard it was very peaceful.
The door of the stable opened on to a
small wooden-fenced paddock.

'Here we are,' Mrs Wakefield
announced. 'I'll let Apple and Currant
out.'

The girls waited by the fence while
Grace's mum opened the stable door and
then stepped back out of the way.

After a moment, a dapple-grey mare
walked out. She had a dished face, big

expressive eyes and a long grey mane. She looked around and then whickered softly over her shoulder. There was an answering whinny and out of the stable trotted a tiny black foal, with long spindly legs, enormous dark eyes and a tail that stuck straight out like a bottlebrush.

He stopped beside his mum and looked curiously at the people by the gate.

'Oh, wow!' Lauren breathed. 'He's gorgeous!'

'Very cute!' Mel agreed.

Grace looked pleased.

The foal's eyes flicked around. There wasn't a trace of fear in his expression; he just looked lively and inquisitive.

'Will he stay black?' Lauren asked, remembering that she'd read somewhere that grey horses were usually born black.

Jade shot her a withering look. 'Of course he'll st—' she started to say at the same time as Grace said:

'We think he'll turn into a grey, don't we, Mum? Black foals usually do.'

Jade hastily corrected herself. 'Of *course* he'll change colour, Lauren.' She made it sound like it had been a really dumb question.

Currant began to walk towards them. As he neared the fence Apple cut in front of him, stopping him from reaching them. She threw her head in the air, as if warning them to stay away.

'She wasn't this protective the first time she had a foal, was she, Mum?' Grace said.

Mrs Wakefield shook her head. 'It's still early days. I'm sure she'll settle down soon.'

Lauren looked at the anxious mare.
'It's all right, girl,' she murmured. 'We
don't want to hurt you or your baby.'

Apple looked at her.

'He's very beautiful,' Lauren told her
softly. 'You must be very proud.'

Apple slowly stretched out her muzzle
towards her. Lauren held out her hand.
Taking a cautious step forward, Apple
sniffed at Lauren's fingers. She blew
down her nose and stared at Lauren
with her big dark eyes.

'Goodness,' said Mrs Wakefield. 'You
should feel very honoured, Lauren. Apart
from me, you're the only person Apple
has approached since Currant's been born.
You must have a real way with horses.'

Lauren felt a glow of pride. She always seemed to get on well with horses, even nervous ones. Jessica and Mel grinned at her but Jade looked cross that Lauren was getting all the attention.

'Well, I'd better be getting back to the yard,' said Mrs Wakefield. 'Stay here as long as you want but please don't try and touch Currant. I don't want Apple to get upset. I'm leaving you in charge, Grace, OK?'

'OK,' said Grace.

Mrs Wakefield headed back to the yard.

'Currant's so cute,' Jade said. She put her hand through the fence. 'Here, boy,' she called.

'Jade, don't,' Grace said quickly. 'You heard what my mum said.'

'Chill out,' Jade said. 'Apple will be fine.' She held out her hand again and clicked her tongue.

'No, Jade!' Grace exclaimed, grabbing her arm. 'Don't be so dumb!'

Jade shook her off. 'I'm not dumb!'

'Well, you're acting that way,' said Grace. She turned to the others. 'Come on. I think we should all go back to the yard. I don't want to risk upsetting Apple.'

'OK,' Lauren said reluctantly. She could see why Grace didn't want to risk staying there with Jade acting the way she was. 'Bye, Apple. Bye, Currant.'

Currant pricked up his ears and suddenly an image flashed into Lauren's mind – a picture of Currant grown up, his coat sparkling white, and a silvery horn on his head.

She stared at Currant's broad forehead and slender legs, at his intelligent face and bold expression. She'd just had an amazing, wonderful thought.

Could Currant possibly, just possibly, be a unicorn in disguise?

CHAPTER
Four

'Lauren, come on!' Mel called.
'Coming!' Lauren shot a last look
at Currant and hurried after her friends.
Her mind was buzzing. Could Currant
really be a unicorn? She knew that
Twilight had been born in a magic land
called Arcadia and that he'd come to live
among humans when he was a year old.
However, she also knew that sometimes

unicorns were born on earth as foals. She couldn't wait to ask Twilight what he thought.

'So how about it, Lauren?' Grace said. 'Are you going to come?'

'Come where?' said Lauren.

'To the Fun Day,' Grace said.

'Fun Day?' Lauren echoed.

'Lauren!' Mel grinned. 'I could tell you weren't listening. Grace was just telling us that her mum is organizing a Fun Day for later this week.'

'It's to help welcome the new people to the stables,' Grace explained. 'There's going to be gymkhana games and a Handy Pony class. Are you interested?'

'Definitely!' A thought struck Lauren. 'But will that be OK? I mean it's not as if we keep our ponies here.'

'It'll be fine,' Grace said. 'Mum wants as many people here as possible.'

'Prince is much too valuable to go charging about in gymkhana games,' said Jade. 'But I suppose I *could* take him in the Handy Pony.'

'Don't force yourself,' Mel muttered. Jade glared at her.

'What happens in a Handy Pony class?' Jessica asked Grace.

'It's a class that tests how safe and obedient a pony is,' Grace explained. 'You have to do things like getting the pony to walk over a plastic sheet, carry a

flag, open and shut a gate while you're
on the pony, and do a few small jumps.
It's really fun.'

'Cool!' Mel said enthusiastically.

They reached the yard. 'I'd better go
and see if Mum needs me to do
anything,' Grace said. 'If you're not busy
tomorrow, why don't you come over in
the morning and practise?'

'I can't,' Mel said regretfully. 'I'm
going to the dentist.'

'And it's my stepsister Samantha's turn
to ride Sandy tomorrow,' Jessica said.

'I can come,' Lauren said.

'All right, I'll see you tomorrow about
ten, Lauren,' Grace said, and she hurried
off.

Lauren turned to Mel and Jessica. 'The Fun Day sounds brilliant, doesn't it?'

Jade smirked. 'It's lucky for you there aren't show classes, Lauren. Twilight's looking scruffier than ever. Don't you *ever* groom him?' She glanced across the yard to where Twilight was standing.

'Yes, actually, I do — *every day*,' Lauren said shortly. She walked over to Twilight.

'Really? You can't tell,' Jade replied, following her.

'Shut up, Jade!' Mel exclaimed.

'Twilight looks a million times better with Lauren than he ever did when you had him!' Jessica said hotly.

Lauren was grateful for her friends' support but she didn't want to get into a quarrel with Jade. 'Let's go,' she said to Mel and Jessica. 'We can ride to the creek and have our picnic.'

Jade frowned, cross at being ignored. 'Just look at Twilight, Lauren,' she went on loudly. 'His mane needs pulling and he's been rubbing his tail and . . .' All of a sudden Twilight sneezed all over Jade's smart black jacket.

Jade gasped. 'Yuck!' she cried, staring at the sticky mess on her sleeve. 'Look what's he done to me! That's gross!'

Lauren couldn't hide her grin. 'Sorry, Jade. You must have been standing too close, but never mind, I'm sure it'll wash off.'

Twilight tossed his head, his eyes gleaming mischievously. Lauren was sure he'd sneezed on purpose. It served Jade right for making mean comments! 'Come on, boy,' she said, patting his neck. 'Let's go for our picnic!'

★

It was fun eating lunch by the creek and letting the ponies paddle in the water. Spring flowers grew along the riverbank and the trees were green with new young leaves. As Lauren munched on a chocolate biscuit, she felt very happy. It was the beginning of the holidays, she had a fun show to look forward to, and there was a possible new unicorn nearby! Not even the memory of Jade's mean words could dent her cheerfulness. She just hoped that Twilight hadn't been upset by what Jade had said.

Beside her, Jessica sighed. 'We should go home. I said I'd be back by two o'clock.' Getting to her feet, she fed the remains of her apple to Sandy.

'All right,' Mel said, picking up her hat and squashing it on to her black curls. 'Let's tack up again.'

They rode home through the woods and stopped when they reached the end of the track where Lauren needed to turn left to ride back to her farm.

'Should we meet on Wednesday morning and get ready for the Fun Day together?' Mel said.

Jessica nodded and Lauren said, 'I'll come round about eight.'

The girls said goodbye and went their separate ways.

As Twilight began to walk down the track towards Granger's Farm, Lauren looked around. She really wanted to talk to him. 'Come on, Twilight,' she said suddenly. 'Let's go to the secret clearing.'

He turned off the path on to an overgrown track that led through the trees. Lauren had to duck low on his neck to avoid the overhanging branches. The path twisted through the trees until it opened into a clearing. Yellow and white butterflies fluttered through the air and the grass was studded with purple and gold flowers.

Lauren said the Turning Spell.

'Hey, there,' Twilight said as he changed into a unicorn. 'Is everything OK?'

Lauren knew he was wondering why she had turned him into a unicorn in the middle of the day. 'I just wanted to

talk to you,' she explained. 'I'm sorry about what Jade said about you being scruffy. Are you upset?'

'Of course not.' Twilight shook his mane. 'I know I'm not the neatest, most beautiful pony in the world, but I don't mind. The other ponies can't fly!'

'You're the most beautiful pony in the world to me,' Lauren said loyally. She sighed. 'Jade's so annoying.'

'It's best just to ignore people like that,' Twilight said.

'I know.' Suddenly Lauren remembered something. 'Oh, Twilight, I think Apple's foal might be a unicorn!'

'Really?' Twilight looked excited.

Lauren told him all about Currant. 'He seemed so intelligent. Is there any way we can tell for sure?' she asked.

'Not definitely,' Twilight said. 'Foals don't find out if they're unicorns until they're one year old but there are usually some clues. It's just the same way as a

human who might be a possible unicorn
friend can be spotted – because they
have a good heart and believe in magic.
Foals who might be unicorns also have
certain qualities – they're usually very
clever and very curious.'

Lauren pictured the foal with his wise expression. 'I really think Currant might be a unicorn!'

Twilight pricked up his ears. 'Well, why don't we visit him? If I see him I might be able to spot some special unicorn-ness about him.'

'OK,' Lauren agreed. 'Let's go tonight!'

That evening, Lauren and Twilight swooped across the dark fields towards Orchard Stables. Lauren grinned as she thought how surprised the cows would be if they looked up and saw Twilight flying through the sky!

They landed in a copse of trees by the foaling stable and Lauren

dismounted. She looked round carefully
in case Mrs Wakefield had decided to
come and do a last check before going
to bed. Grace and her family lived in a
house at the other end of the drive
leading down to the yard.

Everywhere was quiet, so they walked
over to the stable. Apple was lying in the
straw with her eyes closed. Currant was
on his feet, nosing inquisitively around
the stable.

'Currant!' Lauren whispered.

The foal looked up. Seeing Twilight
looking over the door, his eyes widened.
He stared at Twilight's horn as if he
couldn't believe what he was seeing.

Twilight whinnied softly. The foal

walked over and stretched out his
velvety nose. Twilight breathed out softly.

'Hello,' Lauren heard him say. 'I'm
Twilight. I'm a unicorn.'

Currant whickered curiously.

'Yes, a unicorn's like a pony,' Twilight
replied. 'But we have horns on our
heads and we can fly and do magic.'

Currant stamped one tiny hoof and
snorted.

'What's he saying?' Lauren asked.

'He says he'd like to be a unicorn
too.' Twilight turned back to the foal.
'I'm afraid you can't be. At least not yet.
But maybe when you're older.'

'Do you think he will be one?'
Lauren said.

'I think he might.' Suddenly Twilight
tensed. 'Listen!'

'What?' Lauren said.

'I heard a noise outside.' As Twilight
spoke, Lauren noticed that his horn had
started to shine with a silvery light. 'It
sounded like footsteps. Someone's
coming!'

'Quick,' Lauren said in alarm. 'We'd
better go. Bye, Currant!'

They backed away from the stable.
What had Twilight heard? Lauren hoped
it wasn't Grace's mum. Suddenly her
eyes caught sight of a moving shadow.
One of the barn cats was padding down
the path towards the stable, making no
noise at all on its delicate paws.

'It's just a cat.' She turned to Twilight.
'Is that what you heard?'

'Yes!' Realization dawned on Twilight's
face. 'I *knew* it didn't sound like a
human's footsteps.'

'But how did you hear something so
quiet?' Lauren said, looking at him in
amazement.

'I don't know, I just did,' answered
Twilight, looking puzzled.

Lauren noticed his horn was still
shining, and her stomach flipped
over with excitement. 'Maybe it's a
new magic power!' Twilight had
lots of magic powers but he only
found out about them one by
one.

'Yes!' Twilight agreed. 'Wow!' He looked pleased. 'I've got a new power.'

Lauren stroked him. 'It's a really useful one. We'll be able to use it to hear if anyone's sneaking up on us, or to check if anyone's around when we're flying.'

Twilight nuzzled her happily. 'I like it when we find out about new powers.'

'Me too,' grinned Lauren.

She took hold of his mane and swung herself on to his back. As Twilight rose into the air, Lauren looked down at Orchard Stables. She thought about the next day. It was going to be great to practise with Jo-Ann and Grace. Maybe she'd even get to see Currant again. She pictured the curious foal.

I hope he's a unicorn, she thought excitedly. *I really do!*

CHAPTER
Five

'Hi, Lauren!' Jo-Ann called as Lauren rode in to the yard the next morning. Jo-Ann was grooming her pony, Beauty.

'Hi!' Lauren rode over. 'Is it still OK if I come and practise with you?'

'Of course,' Jo-Ann replied. 'But Grace and I have decided we won't actually enter the competition. Mrs Wakefield wants us

to help steward the classes instead. It's fine
by us because we enter loads of shows
already. It will be fun to help out.'

Just then Grace came out of a stable.
'Hello, Lauren. Are you all ready to
practise for the Handy Pony?'

Lauren nodded.

'I need five more minutes to finish
grooming,' Jo-Ann said.

Grace looked at Lauren. 'Do you want
to come and see Currant while we wait?
You can leave Twilight here.'

'OK.'

Lauren tied up Twilight and followed
Grace across the yard.

Apple was eating some hay by the
paddock gate and Currant was standing

beside her. When he saw the two girls, he came towards the fence, but catching the warning look that Apple shot in their direction, Grace and Lauren stayed back.

'I wish we could stroke him,' Grace said. 'It's not like Apple to be aggressive.'

'I guess she just wants to look after her baby,' said Lauren.

Grace smiled. 'I would too if he was mine. He's gorgeous.'

Currant looked at them cheekily from under his mum's neck, then stuck his muzzle in the pile of hay, and tossed his head, sending hay flying into the air. Lauren and Grace giggled. Currant snorted and then pushed his head under Apple's tummy and started to feed.

'He's adorable!' Lauren said.

Grace smiled. 'He is. Come on, let's go and see if Jo's ready to practise.'

Ten minutes later, Lauren, Grace and Jo-Ann rode into the schooling ring. Grace and Jo-Ann had put out a course that was similar to the Handy Pony competition but not exactly the same, because that would be cheating.

'You have to ride through those cones,' Grace said, pointing out a row of six cones. 'Then pick up that flag and carry it to the bucket. Ride over the sheet of plastic, through the gate and then over the three jumps.'

'I'll go first,' said Jo-Ann. Lauren knew Jo-Ann's bay mare, Beauty, was fantastic at jumping. But she didn't seem to like Handy Pony. She spooked at the cones, knocking two over. She wouldn't go near the flag, and stopped dead when she got to the plastic. Jo-Ann talked to her patiently, and eventually Beauty leapt over it as if it was a jump and charged towards the three fences. She cleared them easily.

Jo-Ann rode back to the others.
'Maybe it's a good thing I'm not
entering the Handy Pony class after all,'
she said with a grin. She patted Beauty's
neck. 'Jumping's more your thing, isn't it,
girl?'

Beauty tossed her head.

'My turn next,' said Grace. Her pony, Windfall, was much steadier than Beauty and he went right round the course, only stopping at the plastic. But after a few coaxing words from Grace he stepped over it.

'Well done!' Jo-Ann called.

'That was great,' Lauren said.

Grace looked pleased. 'Thanks. Take your time with the plastic – ponies are often a bit worried by it at first.'

Lauren gathered up her reins. She had no idea how Twilight would behave because she'd never done anything like this with him before.

Twilight seemed to have worked out

what to do. He trotted calmly around the cones, being careful not to touch them, and stopped by the flag so that Lauren could pick it up. Then he walked up to the bucket and waited while she put it down. But he stopped when he reached the plastic sheet and looked down at it, snorting.

'Good boy,' Lauren said, squeezing him on. Twilight put a hoof on the plastic. It rustled and he hesitated. Lauren could tell he was worried. An idea came to her and she dismounted. Holding on to Twilight's reins she walked on to the plastic herself.

'Look,' she said. 'It's fine.' Twilight stared uncertainly at the plastic beneath her feet. She walked over and stroked his nose. 'You know I'd never ask you to do anything that would hurt you. Trust me, Twilight. It's OK.' Twilight put his head down and sniffed at the plastic. Then to Lauren's delight he walked on to it. 'Good boy!' she exclaimed, leading him across to the other side.

She got back on and this time he
trotted over the plastic without hesitating.

Jo-Ann and Grace clapped. 'Well done!'

Twilight flew over the three jumps
and Lauren cantered him back to the
others.

'That was great!' said Jo-Ann. 'It was a
really good idea to get off and lead him
over it.'

'Shall we have another go?' Grace
suggested.

They had each ridden round the
course a few more times when Lauren
saw Jade ride into the ring on Prince.
Lauren groaned to herself.

'Are you practising for the Handy
Pony?' Jade asked them.

Grace nodded.

'I'll practise too,' Jade said. She began
to warm Prince up. It was easy to see
why he had won so many prizes. He
moved with long smooth strides and did
everything Jade asked, going from walk
to trot to canter at the lightest of aids.
Jade was a good rider, although she
seemed very strict, correcting Prince
sharply for the slightest mistake.

At last she started the course. Prince
went brilliantly until he reached the
plastic. He stopped dead about a metre
away from it and stared at it with wide,
scared eyes.

'Walk on!' Jade commanded.

Prince didn't move.

Jade nudged him firmly and when he still didn't move she growled at him. He hesitated and took a tiny step, then changed his mind and ran backwards.

'Just take it slowly,' Grace called.

'I know what to do,' Jade snapped back. She gave Prince a tap with her whip. 'Walk on!'

Jo-Ann jumped off Beauty and handed the reins to Grace. 'Getting cross won't help,' she said, starting to walk towards Jade. 'Here, let me lead him.'

'He can do it!' Jade smacked Prince again.

He leapt forward, landed on the plastic and cantered over it in two bounds.

'There!' Jade said, giving them a

triumphant smile. 'I told you he could do it.'

Lauren glanced at Grace and Jo-Ann. They didn't look impressed.

'Yes, but will he ever go near plastic again?' Grace muttered. She turned to Jo-Ann and Lauren. 'I'm going to take Windfall in now. Are you two coming?'

They nodded. When they got back to the yard, Lauren patted Twilight and dismounted. 'You can have a rest and then we'll go home,' she said.

She gave him a drink and then picked out his feet, being careful to sweep up the mud from his hooves. She didn't want to leave a mess on the yard. She was just putting the broom away when

Jade rode over and tied Prince up next to Twilight.

Lauren went to the tack room and bought a can of lemonade from the drinks machine. When she had finished, she went back to Twilight.

Prince had gone but the place where he had been tied up was covered with bits of mud. Jade had obviously picked out his hooves and not swept up the mess.

Just then Mrs Wakefield came round the corner. She saw the mud and frowned. 'Lauren, could you fetch a broom and clean your mess up please?'

'But the mud's not from Twilight's hooves,' Lauren protested.

'Whose pony is it from then?' asked
Mrs Wakefield.

Lauren hesitated. She didn't like
telling tales. 'Um . . .'

Just then Jade walked round the
corner. 'Lauren! Haven't you cleared up
the mess from Twilight's hooves yet?' She

turned to Grace's mum, her eyes wide. 'I told Lauren we have to clear up after ourselves here, Mrs Wakefield.'

Lauren stared at her in outrage. 'But it's not Twilight's mess!'

'It is,' Jade insisted. 'I saw you picking his feet out.'

'Yes, I did, but I swept the mud up!' Lauren exclaimed. 'It's —'

'OK. Enough!' Mrs Wakefield interrupted them. 'I don't know who made the mess but Lauren, seeing as Twilight is tied up here, would you mind getting a broom and clearing it up for me?'

Lauren nodded glumly. Jade shot her a triumphant grin.

'And Jade,' Mrs Wakefield went on, 'I'd
like you to help Lauren.'

'But –' Jade started to protest.

'*Please*,' Mrs Wakefield repeated in a
steely voice.

Lauren had a feeling Jade hadn't
fooled Grace's mum after all.

Jade seemed to decide not to argue. 'Sure, Mrs Wakefield,' she said, smiling sweetly.

When Grace's mum walked away, Lauren turned crossly to Jade. 'It was your mess all along!'

Jade smirked. 'And now *you've* got to clear it up.'

'You mean *we've* got to,' Lauren said through gritted teeth. 'I'm going to get some brooms.'

She marched over to the barn and fetched two brooms, but when she returned, Jade had gone. The mess, of course, was still there.

Lauren felt like screaming. Could anyone be more annoying than Jade Roberts?

CHAPTER

Six

'Lauren, could you pass the shampoo, please?'

'Sure. Here it is!'

It was the morning of the Fun Day and Lauren, Mel and Jessica were grooming their ponies at Mel's. Lauren scrubbed at Twilight's grass stains with warm soapy water. She wanted him to look as beautiful as possible. She wasn't

going to give Jade any opportunity to
criticize him.

A picture of Twilight in his unicorn
form flashed into her mind. If only Jade
knew what he really looked like! Lauren
grinned as she imagined how jealous
Jade would be if she knew that Twilight
was a unicorn in disguise and that
Lauren was his unicorn friend. The night
before, she and Twilight had spent several
hours swooping through the forest while
he had practised using his new power of
magical hearing. He'd told her
everything he could hear as they had
flown through the trees – the squeak of
a tiny mouse, the rustle of a grey
squirrel in the branches of an oak tree,

the whine of a fox cub as he waited for his mother to return. It had been great fun. Lauren put her arm over Twilight's neck and gave him a hug. She, for one, was very glad that Jade wasn't his unicorn friend!

Next to Twilight, Jessica was washing
Sandy's white socks and Mel was putting
a tail bandage on Shadow. 'I wonder
how we'll do in the classes,' Lauren said
to them.

'Well, I hope we beat Jade after what
she did to you yesterday,' replied Mel.
Lauren had told her friends about Jade's
trick.

'I don't care what she does,' Lauren shrugged. 'I'm just going to ignore her.'

'Me too,' Jessica agreed, and Mel nodded.

When the ponies were gleaming, the girls went to get changed. Lauren had decided to wear her cream jodhpurs and brown jodhpur boots. She didn't have a riding jacket but it was just a fun show so wearing a shirt and jumper would be fine. She braided her hair in a neat plait and put on a pair of black gloves that she had been given for Christmas. They had her name embroidered on the cuffs in small white writing and looked very smart.

I look just fine, she thought, examining her reflection in Mel's bedroom mirror.

She turned to the others. 'Are you ready?'

'I am,' Mel said, jumping up from the bed where she had been putting on her socks.

'So am I,' said Jessica.

Lauren grinned. 'Then let's go!'

A huge banner hung over the gate that led to Orchard Stables. *'Orchard Stables Fun Day!'* it announced.

'Wow!' Lauren exclaimed. 'Doesn't the yard look great?'

There were balloons tied to the gates and strings of paper flags looped over the barn doorways. A refreshment table had been set up at one side of the yard. There were plates of sandwiches, delicious-looking chocolate brownies, and a cake stand piled high with white and yellow cupcakes. A big sign read, 'Please help yourself and don't forget treats for your horse!' An arrow underneath pointed to two buckets, one filled with carrot pieces and one with horse biscuits.

'I vote we head over there,' said Jessica, looking hungrily at the cakes.

'Let's go and put our names down for the classes first,' Lauren said.

They rode towards the table where Jo-Ann and Grace were taking entries for the classes.

'Shall I enter for all of us?' Lauren asked.

'OK,' Mel replied. 'I'll hold Twilight.'

'Hi, Lauren!' Grace called. 'Which classes do you want to enter?'

Lauren grinned. 'Everything!'

Grace started scribbling Lauren's, Mel's and Jessica's names on to the entry sheets. There was going to be a sack race, a flag race, a walk, trot and canter race, and the Handy Pony competition. 'Mum's got a secret idea up her sleeve for the Handy Pony,' Grace told Lauren. 'She always likes thinking of new twists to classes. I like your gloves, by the way,' she added.

'Thanks,' Lauren said. 'I got them for Christmas.' She broke off as she heard a familiar voice.

'You're in my way! I'm trying to get to the gate! Move!'

Jade was riding through the other
ponies towards the gate. Prince's dark bay
coat was gleaming and his two white
socks were spotlessly
clean. Jade was
wearing a smart
black showing jacket
and white
jodhpurs.

She caught
sight of
Lauren. 'I see
you decided
not to dress
up, Lauren.'

Lauren flushed.

'You look fine,' Grace reassured her.

'It's just a Fun Day. There'd be no point in dressing as if you were going to a huge big show.'

Jade frowned.

Just then Mrs Wakefield lifted a loudhailer. 'Please could all the entrants for the gymkhana games come to the ring!'

Lauren hurried back to Twilight. It was time for the Fun Day to begin!

A starting line was marked out with cones at one end of the schooling ring. A row of sacks had been laid out for the first race. Lauren, Mel and Jessica rode into the ring with about fifteen other people. Mrs Wakefield explained that she was going to split them into four groups for each race. The winner of each group would go through to a final to decide the rosettes.

All the races were great fun. There was lots of shouting and laughing as people got tangled up in their sacks, tripped over and dropped flags.

By the time the races were over, Twilight was no longer looking neat and tidy. His mane was sticking up, his legs were speckled with mud and he had damp patches on his neck, but Lauren didn't care. They were having a wonderful time and that was all that mattered!

She rode out of the ring with two rosettes – a second place in the sack race and a third in the walk, trot and canter.

Jessica won the walk, trot and canter, and Mel came third in the flag race and fourth in the sack race.

'Wasn't that cool?' Mel exclaimed as they rode out of the ring, rosettes fluttering on the ponies' bridles.

'It was brilliant,' Lauren agreed.

Jade was sitting on Prince just outside the ring. She looked as though she thought games were too silly for words.

'I think Jade's forgotten this is supposed to be a *fun* day,' Jessica joked.

Lauren and Mel giggled.

In the ring, Grace and Jo-Ann were helping Mrs Wakefield to set up for the Handy Pony competition.

'What do you think Mrs Wakefield's

secret idea is?' Jessica said warily.

'I don't know,' Mel mused. 'The course looks just like Grace and Jo-Ann said it would.'

Mrs Wakefield called the twelve Handy Pony competitors into the ring. 'I thought I'd give all of you riders an extra challenge in this class,' she said with a smile. 'This is supposed to be a day for getting to know each other — and each other's ponies. So instead of this being a Handy Pony class, it's going to be a Handy Rider.'

Lauren glanced at Mel and Jessica. They looked as confused as she was.

'Which means you're going to swap ponies,' Mrs Wakefield went on.

Several people gasped.

'You'll ride someone else's pony around the course,' Grace's mum explained. 'It will be interesting to see how quickly you can form a new partnership with a strange horse. I'll give you all ten minutes to get to know your new ride.' She held up a hat with some pieces of paper inside. 'I've put all your names into this hat. I'm going to ask half of you to pick out a name and then you'll swap with that person. So who wants to go first?'

'I'll go,' Jade said. She fished into the hat and picked out a name.

'Whose name have you got?' said Mrs Wakefield.

Lauren's heart
skipped a beat as
Jade's eyes met hers.
'Lauren Foster,'
Jade announced.
'I'm going to
be riding
Twilight.'

CHAPTER
Seven

L auren gasped.

'OK, Lauren and Jade swap ponies,' said Mrs Wakefield. 'Someone else's turn to choose a name.'

Jade led Prince over. 'I can't believe I've got to ride Twilight while you get to ride Prince,' she hissed. 'It's not fair. You'll do really well because Prince is brilliant compared with Twilight.'

'Twilight's just as good,' Lauren said angrily. Shooting Twilight an apologetic look, she handed his reins to Jade. He nudged her with his nose as if to say that he didn't mind.

Jade swung herself on to Twilight's back. Not even bothering to pat him, she rode away and began cantering around the ring.

Lauren decided to take a moment to get to know Prince. 'Hi, boy,' she murmured, patting him. 'I'm Lauren.'

Prince was a very handsome pony with a dished face and big dark eyes. He lifted his muzzle to her face and blew out. Lauren knew it was his way of saying hello.

She stood there for a few minutes, talking quietly to him. On the other side of the ring, Jessica was getting on to a pony called Lemonade, while Mel had a stocky skewbald called Ziggy.

'Ride around for a few minutes to get to know your new pony and then we'll start,' Mrs Wakefield called.

Lauren quickly realized that Prince was very well schooled and eager to please. *No wonder Jade does so well on him,* she thought, as they jumped a small cross-pole.

'What's he like to ride?' Mel asked, trotting up on Ziggy.

'Fantastic,' Lauren replied, smiling. She watched Jo-Ann lay a piece of plastic sheeting next to the practice fence. 'I'm going to take Prince over that. He didn't seem to like it much yesterday.'

She rode Prince towards it, aware that Jade was watching her closely. Prince hesitated when he saw the plastic and then stopped. Lauren coaxed him gently with her voice but he wouldn't move.

'You'll need to be firmer than that if you want to get him to walk over the plastic,' Jade called.

Lauren ignored her. 'Come on, boy,' she said. Prince still wouldn't move so she did what she'd done the day before with Twilight and dismounted.

'I can't believe you're getting off,' Jade said scornfully. 'Don't you know anything about horses? You have to *make* them do what you want – show them who's the boss.'

Lauren continued to ignore her. After a lot of patting and talking to him encouragingly, she got Prince to walk over the plastic. At first he jogged nervously, lifting his hooves high, but after Lauren had led him over it three times he began to calm down. Lauren mounted and Prince let her ride him across it without a fuss.

'Good boy!' Lauren praised him.

Jade scowled.

'OK, everyone!' Mrs Wakefield called. 'It's time for the first competitor, Jessica Parker riding Lemonade.'

Jessica rode into the ring. Lemonade was a long-legged steel-grey pony who looked quite excitable. He fidgeted with the reins and jogged, but Jessica rode him very patiently and he only made a few mistakes – knocking over one of the cones and refusing to stand still at the gate while she closed it.

'Well done, Jessica. That was a very good round,' announced Mrs Wakefield. 'Now for our second competitor, Lauren Foster riding Prince!'

Prince trotted neatly through the cones and halted by the barrel. Lauren picked up the water bottle but as she was carrying it towards the second barrel it slipped through her fingers and she

had to dismount to pick it up. She heard
Jade laughing from the gate. Red in the
face, she remounted. The rest of the
round went much more smoothly.
Prince stood like a statue while Lauren
opened and shut the gate and although
he hesitated as they approached the
plastic, he walked over it without a fuss
when Lauren patted his neck. He cleared
all three jumps easily at the end.

'Good round, Lauren!' Mrs Wakefield
called as everyone clapped. 'Next we
have Jade Roberts riding Twilight.'

As Lauren rode out, Jade hissed,
'Prince only did well because I've
schooled him! You shouldn't think it was
anything to do with your riding.'

Shortening her reins, she pushed Twilight into a trot. Twilight tucked his nose in, looking uncomfortable. Lauren usually rode him with a very light contact. But he was very well-mannered and halted squarely by the barrels and the gate.

As Jade rode him up to the plastic sheet, she gave him a tap on his shoulder with her whip. Twilight swished his tail in protest but walked over the plastic. However, from the way his ears were laid back, Lauren could tell that he wasn't impressed with being smacked for no reason.

Jade turned him towards the jumps. 'Canter on!'

Lauren saw a mischievous look suddenly cross Twilight's face. Jade sat down in the saddle and tried to push him into a canter but Twilight just slowed down.

Jade's heels flapped and she smacked Twilight again but it had no effect. He slowed to a jog and then to a walk.

Reaching the first jump, he stopped
right in front of it.

A few of the spectators giggled. 'I
think Twilight's doing it on purpose,' Mel
whispered. 'You can tell from his face.'

Lauren had to agree. There was a very
cheeky look in Twilight's eyes.

Jade raised her whip. Suddenly Twilight
leapt over the fence from a standstill.

'Whoaa!' Jade cried, her arms flailing.
As Twilight landed on the other side, she
fell forwards on to his neck. For a
moment Lauren thought Twilight was
going to put his head down so that Jade
would slither off. But he didn't. Instead
he lifted his neck and slid her safely
back into the saddle.

Jade wasn't hurt and everyone burst
out laughing. But Jade didn't see the
funny side. Grabbing the reins, she
yanked at Twilight's mouth and lifted her
whip again.

'Jade!' Mrs Wakefield exclaimed,
starting to walk towards her.

Lauren was quicker. Throwing Prince's reins to Mel, she raced across the ring. 'Stop it, Jade!' she shouted.

Jade swung herself off Twilight's back. 'You're welcome to him. He's a useless pony and you're a useless rider, Lauren Foster!'

'He is *not* useless!' Lauren exploded.

'He is. He's –'

'That will do, Jade,' said Mrs Wakefield. 'Lauren, maybe you'd better take Twilight in.'

Lauren nodded. She rubbed Twilight's nose. 'You're *not* useless,' she told him shakily.

'No, he's not,' said Mrs Wakefield, giving him a pat. 'Only bad riders ever blame

their horse, Jade,' she said. 'I think you
need to go and cool down for a while.'

Red in the face, Jade marched away.

'OK,' Mrs Wakefield said. 'Jade
Roberts has retired on Twilight. Can we
have the next competitor in the ring,
please? That's Lindsey Huston on Rusty.'

Lauren led Twilight out of the ring.
'Are you OK?' she murmured. 'I'm
really sorry I let Jade ride you.'

He pushed her with his nose and gave
her a cheeky sideways look.

Seeing the mischievous glint in his
eye, Lauren felt a glimmer of relief. She
had a feeling Twilight was saying he
thought Jade was even more sorry!

As soon they got out of the ring Mel,

Jessica, Grace and Jo-Ann surrounded them.

'Poor Twilight,' said Jessica, stroking him.

'Jade's such an idiot!' Mel exclaimed.

'I couldn't believe it when she almost hit him,' said Grace.

Lauren caught sight of Jade walking past with Prince's saddle. It was obvious she'd heard the comments. Her face went white and, biting her lip, she hurried away.

Lauren hesitated. The last thing she felt like doing was comforting Jade, but she also knew how horrid it was to hear yourself being talked about.

Twilight nudged her with his nose and Lauren realized he'd seen Jade too.

She made up her mind. 'Can you hold
Twilight for a minute?' she said to Mel.

Lauren caught up with Jade at the
tack-room door.

Jade swung round. 'What do you want?'

'I . . . I just wanted to say I'm sorry
you heard that stuff the others were
saying,' Lauren said awkwardly.

'Yeah, right!' Jade spat. 'You think
you're so cool, with all your friends
telling you how wonderful you are, don't
you, Lauren? Well, you'd better watch
out. People might not be thinking you're
so great for much longer.'

Dumping her saddle on a rack, she
marched off.

Lauren stared after her. What had Jade
meant? Feeling uneasy, she walked back
to the others.

'Where did you go?' Mel asked,
handing her Twilight's reins.

'Nowhere,' Lauren said. Not wanting
to think about it any more, she said,
'Come on, let's go and watch the rest of
the Handy Pony.'

CHAPTER

Eight

The Handy Pony competition
finished without any more drama.
Lauren was placed third for her round
on Prince. Mel came second for an
almost perfect round on Ziggy, and
Jessica was fifth.

'You've all done really well today,'
Grace said to them.

'It's been fantastic,' Mel said happily.

'Yeah,' Jessica agreed, patting Sandy.
'Everyone seemed to enjoy themselves.'

Apart from Jade, Lauren thought. 'Can
we see Currant before we go?' she said
out loud.

'Sure,' Grace said. 'Come on.'

They tied the ponies up and left their
hats and gloves in a pile, then set off
towards the foaling stable. As they were
passing the water trough, they met
Grace's mum. 'Are you going to see
Currant?' she asked.

When they nodded, she said, 'Well, be
very careful of Apple. She seemed very
restless this morning. Don't go into the
stable.'

'We won't,' they promised.

Mrs Wakefield smiled. 'Thank you. I know I can trust all of you.'

As she turned to walk away, Lauren noticed Jade standing by the trough. She had a strange expression on her face.

A shiver of unease ran down Lauren's spine. She was sure Jade was planning another mean trick. Trying not to worry about it she headed after the others.

Currant and Apple were in their
stable. Apple was lying down and
Currant was curled up next to her.
When the girls looked over the door,
Apple got to her feet and stood
protectively over Currant.

'It's all right, beauty,' Lauren
murmured. 'No one's going to hurt you.'

The dapple-grey mare's ears flickered.

'She seems to like you, Lauren,' said
Grace.

'She does but I bet she's still not
going to let us close enough to see
Currant,' Jo-Ann said. 'Come on, let's go
back to the yard.'

Lauren was reluctant to leave. Apple
did seem to be responding to her.

Maybe if she could keep talking to her for a bit longer, the mare would calm down.

The others were already heading up the path. 'Come on, Lauren!' Grace called.

'Coming!' Lauren ran after them.

When they reached the ponies, Lauren, Mel and Jessica began to put their hats and gloves back on.

'Where's my right glove?' Lauren said.

'It must be here,' Jessica said in surprise.

They searched around but there was no sign of it anywhere.

'Don't worry,' said Jo-Ann. 'I'm sure it'll turn up.'

Feeling upset, Lauren got on to
Twilight. She couldn't believe she'd lost
one of her new gloves the first time
she'd worn them.

'Don't worry,' Jessica said, seeing
Lauren's face. 'Your glove's bound to
turn up. No one would steal it. After all,
who'd want a glove with *Lauren Foster*
written on it?'

'I suppose that's true,' Lauren said, feeling a bit more cheerful. She patted Twilight's neck and, sitting back in the saddle, she let him walk on a loose rein all the way home.

That night, Lauren's parents had friends over for supper. As soon as all the adults were settling down at the dinner table, Lauren crept outside. She wanted to talk to Twilight about the show.

'Wasn't Jade impossible today?' she said when she had turned him into a unicorn.

'A bit,' Twilight admitted, nuzzling her arm. 'But I think she got more than she bargained for when she picked me for the Handy Pony. And maybe it will stop her being mean to you,' he added hopefully.

'I doubt it.' Lauren frowned. She told Twilight what Jade had said afterwards. 'She made it sound like she was planning on doing something horrid.' Not wanting to think about it any more, she changed the subject. 'I wish I hadn't lost my glove today.'

'We could always go back to the stables and have another look for it,' Twilight suggested. 'Everyone will have gone home by now.'

'I guess we could,' Lauren agreed. 'You could land by Currant's field and wait in the trees for me. We could take your

saddle and bridle, then if I do meet
anyone, I'll just say I rode you over
there.'

'Good idea,' Twilight said.

Lauren hurried to get her tack. It was
a bit strange to tack Twilight up when he
was a unicorn – she never usually used a

saddle and bridle on him when he was in his magical form. She had to unbuckle the bridle to get it on over his horn.

When he was ready, they flew across the fields. The yard was in darkness, with the only light coming from the Wakefields' house at the end of the drive.

'It doesn't look as if there's anyone around,' Lauren whispered as Twilight swooped towards the trees by the foaling stable.

'I can use my new hearing power to check!' Twilight said excitedly.

He landed on the grass at the edge of the trees and concentrated hard. Lauren saw his horn start to glow with a silver light.

Suddenly Twilight stiffened. 'I can hear someone's voice!' he said in surprise.

'Do you think it's Mrs Wakefield?'

'I don't know. It sounds like a girl. It sounds as if she's saying, "go away".' Twilight listened hard and then looked at Lauren in alarm. 'Whoever it is, I think she's in the foaling stable and it sounds like she's in trouble!'

'In the foaling stable!' Lauren gasped.

'I can't go over there like this,' Twilight said. 'You go and have a look.'

'OK.' Scrambling off his back, Lauren raced over to the stable. As she got nearer she could hear a frightened voice.

'Go away, Apple! Please, go away!'

Lauren stood on tiptoes and looked through the window. Apple was standing with her ears flattened and her neck stretched towards a person who was cowering against the wall.

Lauren gasped. It was Jade!

CHAPTER
Nine

Apple snapped her teeth, missing Jade's arms by millimetres. Jade pressed against the wall with a frightened cry. She was holding something, but Lauren couldn't make out what it was.

Lauren ran back to Twilight. 'It's Jade!' she panted 'She's in the stable and can't get out. We've got to help her. Can you talk to Apple? Persuade her to leave Jade alone?'

Twilight shook his head. 'If I do that Jade will see me. Maybe you should go and get Mrs Wakefield.'

'There isn't time,' Lauren said desperately. 'Apple is really upset.'

'Then *you'll* have to help,' Twilight said.

'Me?' Lauren exclaimed. 'But what can I do?'

'Well, you can't talk to Apple like I'd be able to,' Twilight said, 'but you're really good with horses. You might be able to calm her down, or at least distract her enough so Jade can escape.'

Lauren wasn't sure. She knew Apple was only trying to protect her tiny foal, but she'd looked so fierce!

'You can do it, Lauren,' Twilight urged.

'But . . . but . . .' Lauren stammered.

Twilight touched her face with his muzzle. 'You *have* to do it, Lauren. Jade could get hurt.' He lowered his horn. As it touched Lauren's shoulder, she felt strength and courage flowing into her.

'OK,' she said, taking a deep breath. 'I'll try.'

'Turn me into a pony first,' Twilight told her. 'Then if you need help I can do something without anyone seeing me as a unicorn.'

Lauren quickly said the Undoing Spell. As Twilight turned back into a pony he nudged her with his nose and pushed her gently towards the stable.

Heart pounding, Lauren ran across the grass.

'Lauren!' Jade gasped as Lauren opened the door.

Apple tossed her head at Lauren. 'It's all right, girl,' Lauren murmured. She knew that horses picked up on emotions very easily so it was important she didn't appear frightened. 'Jade's not going to hurt Currant.'

Apple stared suspiciously at her.

Lauren edged into the stable. 'Easy now.' She turned sideways, hoping it would make her seem less threatening.

'Hurry up, Lauren!' Jade exclaimed. 'Get me out of here!'

Apple tensed.

'Be quiet, Jade!' Lauren said. 'I'm trying to help but you need to stay calm.'

Outside the stable, Twilight whinnied encouragingly.

Knowing he was there made Lauren feel better. Twilight would never have suggested she try and calm Apple if he'd thought she wouldn't be able to do it. *I'm not going to let him down*, she thought determinedly.

She looked at the mare. She needed to distract Apple so Jade could escape.

Lauren felt in the pocket of her jeans
and found a half-eaten packet of mints.

Moving slowly, she pulled out the
packet. 'Here, Apple,' she murmured.
'Yummy mints.' She held out her hand,
making sure she didn't look directly at
the mare. She'd read in one of her pony
magazines that looking straight at a
frightened horse would scare it even
more.

For a long moment nothing happened.
Suddenly the straw rustled as Apple took
a step towards her. A second later, Lauren
felt Apple's muzzle tickle her hand.

'Good girl,' Lauren murmured as
Apple crunched up the mint.

Moving very slowly, she took another

mint from the packet. 'When I say so,
walk very quietly out of the stable,'
Lauren whispered to Jade.

'OK,' Jade said faintly.

Lauren held out the second mint.
Apple came closer and crunched it up.

'Now!' Lauren whispered to Jade.

Jade started to edge along the wall.
Apple immediately pinned back her ears
and swung round. Jade froze.

'It's OK, Apple,' Lauren murmured.
Her heart was thudding but she forced
herself to sound calm. 'Here you go,
have another mint.'

She rustled the wrapper. Apple
lowered her head and turned back to
Lauren. With a sigh of relief, Jade
escaped through the stable door.

Lauren fed the last mint to Apple and
then backed out of the stable. Shutting
the door behind her, she leant against it
for a moment, feeling shaky. Twilight
stepped forward and pushed his head
against her. Lauren stroked him with a

trembling hand. Twilight couldn't talk to her because he was in his pony form, but she knew he was telling her she'd done really well.

Jade was sitting on the ground, looking very white.

'Are you all right?' Lauren asked.

Jade nodded.

'What were you doing in there?' Lauren said. 'You know we've been told not to go into Apple's stable. And why were you here when it was dark anyway?'

Jade's face flushed and her fingers curled over the thing she was holding in her hand. It was black and looked like it was made of material. Lauren saw some white writing at the edge.

'What's that?' she demanded.

Jade looked guilty. 'It's . . . well, it's your glove.'

'My glove!' Lauren echoed in astonishment.

'Yes. I picked it up when you left it in the yard today.' Jade bit her lip. 'I . . .

I was going to leave it in the stable so
that Mrs Wakefield would think you'd
been in there with Currant.'

'What?' Lauren exclaimed. Beside her,
Twilight snorted and stamped his hoof
angrily.

Jade hung her head. 'I wanted you to
get into trouble,' she muttered. She
looked up and saw the shock on
Lauren's face. 'I'm sorry. I really am.
Thank you for rescuing me, Lauren. You
were amazing with Apple just now.'

Lauren was stunned. How could Jade
have planned to do something so mean?
She would have been in real trouble if
Mrs Wakefield had found her glove in
the stable.

'So why were you here?' Jade asked.

'I wanted to look for my glove.'
Suddenly Lauren noticed that Twilight
was scraping at the ground with his hoof
as if he was trying to tell her something.
A second later, she heard the sound of
someone walking down the path.

A torch swept through the darkness.
'Who's there?' Mrs Wakefield's voice
called sharply.

'It's Mrs Wakefield!' Jade gasped.

Lauren stared at her in alarm. 'Oh no!
What's she going to say when she finds
us here?'

CHAPTER

Ten

Mrs Wakefield walked towards the stable. When the beam of her torch landed on Lauren and Jade, she stopped. 'What are you two doing here?'

'I . . . er . . . well . . .' Jade stammered.

'Yes?' Mrs Wakefield prompted.

'Well, I came to the stable because . . .' Jade looked down at the glove in her

hand and swallowed. 'Because . . .' Her
voice trailed off.

'I'm waiting for an explanation,' said
Mrs Wakefield, face frowning.

Lauren thought hard. She knew
Grace's mum would be very angry if she
learned the real reason for Jade's visit to

the stable, and despite what Jade had
done, Lauren didn't want her to get into
that much trouble. 'You came because
you offered to help me find my glove,
didn't you, Jade?' she said. She didn't like
lying to Mrs Wakefield but it was the
only way to help Jade.

Jade looked at Lauren in surprise.

'I called Jade,' Lauren went on. 'I
wanted to know if she'd seen my
missing glove. Jade said she thought she'd
seen it near Apple's stable and offered to
come and help me look for it.'

Jade shot Lauren an intensely grateful
look. 'Yes, that's right. And . . . and we
found it, didn't we?' She held up the
glove.

Lauren nodded.

'I see,' Mrs Wakefield said slowly. She didn't sound convinced, but to Lauren's relief she didn't question them further. 'Well, you shouldn't have come back here at night-time on your own.'

'We're sorry,' Jade said.

'Yes. It won't happen again,' Lauren
promised.

'There's no harm done, I suppose,' said
Grace's mum. 'But you two had better
go straight home now. Will you be all
right on your own, Lauren?'

'I'll be fine,' Lauren answered. 'It's
only ten minutes away and Twilight
knows the way really well.'

'How about you, Jade? How did you
get here?' Mrs Wakefield asked.

'On my bike,' Jade replied.

'Have you got lights for it?'

'No,' Jade admitted.

'Then I'd better run you home in my
car,' said Mrs Wakefield. She went to the
door and looked over it. 'At least Apple

and Currant seem OK. Come on, let's go, Jade.'

'See you soon,' Lauren said to Jade.

'Yes,' Jade said, and for the first time ever she gave Lauren a warm smile. 'Thanks, Lauren. For *everything*,' she added in a low voice.

Lauren smiled back. There was no way Jade would ever be a friend like Jessica or Mel, but maybe their days of being enemies were over. She had a feeling that Jade wouldn't be mean to her or Twilight again soon. 'See you,' she said, and she led Twilight towards the trees.

When Mrs Wakefield and Jade had left, she turned him back into a unicorn.

'What did you think of all that?' she exclaimed.

'I can't believe Jade was going to leave your glove in the stable,' Twilight said.

'I know. I found it hard to decide whether to help her when Mrs Wakefield was asking her why she was here,' Lauren admitted. 'Part of me didn't want to, but I didn't want her to get into loads of trouble either.'

Twilight nuzzled her. 'You did the right thing. I think she'd had enough of a shock already.'

'Yes,' Lauren agreed. She frowned as she thought of the mare. 'Apple seems so upset at the moment. I know she's only trying to protect Currant but it's not like anyone is going to hurt him. I wish we could make her understand that . . .' She broke off as an idea flashed through her mind. 'Hang on. Maybe you . . .'

'Maybe I could talk to her!' Twilight exclaimed at the same time.

Lauren grinned. 'That's just what I was going to say.'

They went back to the stable. When
Lauren opened the door, Currant and
Apple turned their heads in alarm.
Seeing Twilight looking like a unicorn,
Currant gave a whinny of recognition
and trotted over.

Lauren tensed as she waited for Apple
to shoo him back. But Apple didn't. To
Lauren's surprise, she whinnied and blew
down her nose at Twilight. He greeted
her in the same way.

Apple whickered softly.

'What's she saying?' Lauren demanded.

'That she was expecting me,' Twilight
said, looking surprised.

Apple whickered again. 'Oh, I
understand now,' said Twilight. He

turned to Lauren. 'Ever since Currant was born, Apple has been waiting for a unicorn to visit. It's because she thinks Currant might be a unicorn foal – just like we do.'

'Is that why she's been extra-protective?' Lauren asked.

'Yes. She's afraid someone might try and hurt him or take him away from her.'

'Oh, Apple,' said Lauren. 'Mrs Wakefield would never let anyone do that. Currant's secret is safe.'

Twilight nuzzled the mare. 'Lauren's right. No one at Orchard Stables would ever do anything to hurt Currant. You won't know whether Currant's a unicorn until he's a year old, when a

Unicorn Elder will visit him. Until then you can treat him like a normal foal.'

Apple snorted in relief.

'Is she going to be OK with people handling Currant now?' Lauren asked.

Apple whinnied.

'Yes,' Twilight interpreted. 'In fact, she says you can stroke him now if you like.'

Feeling very honoured, Lauren stepped forwards. She rubbed Currant's fluffy neck and he twisted his head round to nibble her sleeve.

'Hey!' she said, gently pushing his muzzle away. 'No biting, silly!'

Currant looked at her mischievously and blinked his long eyelashes.

Lauren giggled and stroked Currant's

soft nose. 'I hope you *are* a unicorn,' she murmured. 'Perhaps Grace will be your unicorn friend. She would be perfect and it would be brilliant to be able to share the secret with her. But I suppose we'll just have to wait to find out.'

Currant stepped away and butted his head underneath Apple's belly. Apple nuzzled his hindquarters with a contented sigh.

Lauren smiled. It was a very peaceful scene. 'Come on, let's leave them,' she whispered to Twilight.

They crept out of the stable. It was very dark now. As the stars shone down, Lauren gave Twilight a hug. 'I'm glad we've been able to help calm Apple.'

'So am I.' He rubbed his head against
her. 'And I'm glad we helped Jade, too.
You were amazing.'

'I couldn't have done it without you,'
Lauren told him. 'You made me believe I
could calm Apple down. I don't think
I could have gone into the stable if you
hadn't been there.'

'And I couldn't have got her out of

the stable on my own.' Twilight pushed
her with his nose. 'I guess that's why
unicorns have unicorn friends – you can
do things that I can't and I can do
things that you can't. We help each other
help other people.'

Lauren realized he was right. Whatever
problems they were facing – from
rescuing Jade from the stable to cheering
Buddy up – they solved the problems
they faced together. She stroked his
mane. 'We're a team, aren't we?'

Twilight nodded. 'We are.' He blew
softly on her hair. 'I like us being a
team, Lauren.'

Feeling very happy, Lauren put her
arms around him. 'Me too,' she smiled.

Do you love magic, unicorns and fairies?

Join the sparkling

My Secret Unicorn

fan club today!

It's FREE!

You will receive a sparkle pack, including:

Stickers **Badge**
Membership card **Glittery pencil**

Plus four Linda Chapman newsletters every year,
packed full of fun, games, news and competitions.
And look out for a special card on your birthday!

How to join:

Visit mysecretunicorn.co.uk and enter your details

Send your name, address, date of birth* and email address (if you have one) to:
**Linda Chapman Fan Club, Puffin Marketing,
80 Strand, London, WC2R 0RL**

Your details will be kept by Puffin only for the purpose of sending information regarding Linda Chapman
and other relevant Puffin books. It will not be passed on to any third parties.
You will receive your free introductory pack within 28 days

*If you are under 13, you must get permission from a parent or guardian

Notice to parent/guardian of children under 13 years old: Please add the following to their email/letter including
your name and signature: I consent to my child/ward submitting his/her personal details as above.

Magnificent MABEL
and the Christmas Elf

Ruth
Quayle

Julia
Christians

First published in the UK in 2020 by Nosy Crow Ltd
The Crow's Nest, 14 Baden Place,
Crosby Row, London SE1 1YW

Nosy Crow and associated logos are trademarks and/or registered
trademarks of Nosy Crow Ltd

Text © Ruth Quayle, 2020
Illustrations © Julia Christians, 2020

The right of Ruth Quayle and Julia Christians to be identified as
the author and illustrator respectively of this work has been asserted by them
in accordance with the Copyright, Designs and Patents Act, 1988

1 3 5 7 9 10 8 6 4 2

A CIP catalogue record for this book is available from the British Library

Printed and bound in the UK by Clays Ltd, Elcograf S.p.A.

Papers used by Nosy Crow are made from wood grown in
sustainable forests.

ISBN: 978 1 78800595 1

www.nosycrow.com

MIX
Paper from
responsible sources
FSC® C018072